# ALSO BY ANTHONY C. DELAUNEY

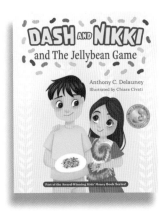

*Dash and Nikki and the Jellybean Game*
(Book 1 in the Owning the Dash Kids' Book series)

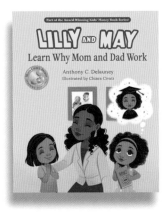

*Lilly and May Learn Why
Mom and Dad Work*
(Book 2 in the Owning the Dash Kids' Book series)

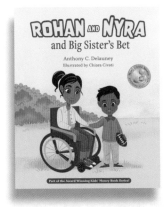

*Rohan and Nyra and Big Sister's Bet*
(Book 3 in the Owning the Dash
Kids' Book series)

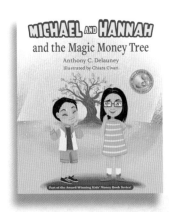

*Michael and Hannah and the Magic
Money Tree*
(Book 4 in the Owning the Dash
Kids' Book series)

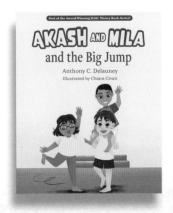

*Akash and Mila and the Big Jump*
(Book 5 in the Owning the Dash
Kids' Book series)

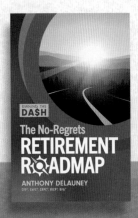

*Owning the Dash:
The No-Regrets Retirement Roadmap*

*Owning the Dash: Applying the Mindset of a Fitness
Master to the Art of Family Financial Planning*

# DEAR READER,

*Akash and Mila and the Big Jump* is the first Owning the Dash Kids' Book to discuss judgment and how it influences decision making. Having worked as a financial planner with families for over two decades, I have discovered that fear of judgment is the most significant roadblock preventing individuals from pursuing their personal, professional, and financial goals. We fear judgment from our friends, our co-workers, our teachers, our family, and especially ourselves. Both of my adult self-help books directly discuss this issue in their opening chapters.

I chose not to tie money to fear of judgment in this book because of the young reader audience. Teaching children at an early age to associate fear of judgment with money can cause more harm than good. The lesson on judgment is essential for parents to discuss with their children, but using examples that children can better understand will prepare them for when they do have to start making decisions with money later in life.

I hope you and your family enjoy the story!

To Akash and Rujuta. Thank you for bringing so much joy into the world and for helping me share this story and its message!

www.amplifypublishinggroup.com

*Akash and Mila and the Big Jump*

For more information, please contact:
Mascot Kids, an imprint of Amplify Publishing Group
620 Herndon Parkway, Suite 220
Herndon, VA 20170
info@mascotbooks.com

Library of Congress Control Number: 2023914999

CPSIA Code: PRKF1023A
ISBN-13: 978-1-63755-860-7

Printed in China

# AKASH AND MILA

## and the Big Jump

Anthony C. Delauney

Illustrated by Chiara Civati

Anthony C Delay
05-03-2024

Today was the day! A stupendously special day
for two best of best friends who loved to jump, run, and play.
They knew what awaited beyond those towering doors.
They could hear the booming thuds of feet flopping on floors.

Cheers rang out from inside. The glass windows fogged with dust.
Akash and Mila could not wait. "Let's go," they both fussed.
They pulled on their parents' arms as they entered to see
gymnasts sprint, spring, and leap nearly as high as a tree.

There were athletes of all ages, looks, shapes, and sizes.
The walls were glittered with trophies, banners, and prizes.
Girls twirled up on a balance beam. Boys flipped on a mat.
A coach flew off the high bar as his team calmly sat.

The best friends didn't notice. They were waving *hello*
to a young boy gymnast whom they both happened to know.
The boy cartwheeled over to them and reached for a hug.
"Glad you made it." He grinned as he gripped them nice and snug.

"Dash, that was too cool!" Akash said, reaching 'round his waist.
"It's your big day," Dash cheered. "You're going to love this place!"
"Do we just watch?" Mila muttered, unsure what to do.
Dash laughed. "No, your coach has something fun prepared for you.

You get to try out the vault. That event is so sweet!
Just make sure that when you land, it's on both of your feet."
Dash waved to the coach, and then he told them where to go.
Akash ran right over, while Mila moved somewhat slow.

"Welcome," the coach said as the new students joined the class.
"Today I'll show a skill that all gymnasts need to pass.
You will each jump off the springboard and land with a pose.
I expect to see arms up and some straight, pointed toes."

One gymnast demonstrated as she sailed through the air.
She looked like a pencil, except with long, flowing hair.
Mila's eyes popped seeing how high the board made her fly.
Akash quickly raised his hand. "May I please have a try?"

"Yes, you can," the coach said, showing Akash where to stand.
"You'll need to start with a run before you jump and land."
Akash couldn't wait. He bolted fast toward the board.
He jumped on the springs. The kids watched as his body soared.

He looked like a superhero, his hands stretching high.
Mila thought he might zoom straight off up into the sky,
but as his body made its way back down to the ground,
Akash fell flat on his belly. No one made a sound.

Mila rushed over to him. "Akash, are you okay?"

Akash looked around, wondering what the kids would say.

His eyes started to tear as he trudged back to his seat.

Mila sat down next to him. They both stared at their feet.

The other gymnasts each had a chance to take their turn.
Mila was last in line. She showed a look of concern.
"May I skip this time?" she asked. The coach did not refuse.
"Absolutely," she said. "You can try one when you choose."

Akash and Mila watched as the others tried again.
Their smiles faded to frowns with a sniffle now and then.
The coach told some jokes to try to help them feel better.
Mila thought they might leave, but Akash would not let her.

Just as it seemed they were both ready to walk away,
two arms wrapped around their shoulders. "Having fun today?"
Dash had wandered over to them from across the room.
"I saw your faces looking full of sadness and gloom."

**B**oth Akash and Mila struggled to show him a smile.
"We aren't good at this," Akash whimpered after a while.
Dash said, "I've seen you both jump so many times before.
Akash, you tried once. Do you want to try for one more?"

"No," Akash replied. "Not with everyone watching me."

"They will laugh at us," Mila cried. "You just wait and see."

Dash paused and sat between them. He then waved to a friend.

"I understand," he said, "and I won't try to pretend."

Dash made an introduction: "This is my friend, Lulu.
I felt like you both when I started gymnastics too.
Lulu was better than me. She did her skills so well.
I could not keep up with her, and everyone could tell.

My first month in the gym, I would see her every day.
I feared showing up. I even almost ran away.
Then one practice we were each trying our floor routine.
I made a big mistake and thought she'd say something mean."

"But Lulu surprised me. She said something very kind.
Her words I'll never forget; they are stuck in my mind.
She helped me up and rested her hand on my shoulder.
'You will be amazing,' she said, 'when you get older.'"

Lulu laughed. "That's right. Dash always pushed to do his best.
He tried and made lots of mistakes, just like all the rest.
He thought he was alone, being judged by the others,
so I told him that *here* we're all sisters and brothers."

"We support each other, and we will support you too. We do not judge anyone. We want the best for you." Dash wiped Akash's tears as Lulu grabbed Mila's hand. "Making mistakes is okay. We know they're never planned.

But now you get to choose. Do you want to try again?
We'll support you no matter what happens in the end."
Akash stood up and said, "I will try at least once more."
All the gymnasts clapped and cheered as he jogged to the floor.

Akash sprinted to the board and sprung up like a star.
He landed on his feet. Shouts roared out from near and far!

Mila was up next. Lulu gave her some tips to try.
She performed a perfect jump with fingers pointing high.

The team gathered 'round Mila. Practice came to a close.
Akash goofed off with Dash while Mila twirled on her toes.
Dash said, "I hope you now see how great this place can be."
"We do," they both replied. "It feels just like family!"

# A VERY BIG THANKS

to Buddy, Debra, Theresa, Coach Tara, Coach Addikus, Michelle, Rohan, Kenzie, Maria, Adam, Gwen, Victoria, Hudson, Ellie, Selena, and all the other incredible gymnasts at TRIumph Gymnastics!

# ABOUT THE AUTHOR

Anthony C. Delauney is a financial advisor based in Raleigh, North Carolina, who has a passion for helping families. He is the founder of Owning the Dash, LLC, an organization dedicated to helping educate and inspire families as they work to achieve their financial goals.

*Akash and Mila and the Big Jump* is Anthony's fifth book in the Owning the Dash Kids' Books series. Anthony wrote this book to entertain children of all ages and to teach them an important lesson that will help guide them in the years to come. Many more fun adventures await all the children in the Owning the Dash Kids' Books series!

## ENJOY THE BOOK? PLEASE LEAVE A REVIEW.

Goodreads

Amazon